WOODY AND JUNE VERSUS TWO GUNS

WOODY AND JUNE VERSUS TWO GUNS

WOODY AND JUNE VERSUS THE APOCALYPSE, EPISODE 9

ROBERT J. MCCARTER

LITTLE HUMMINGBIRD PUBLISHING

WOODY AND JUNE VERSUS THE APOCALYPSE

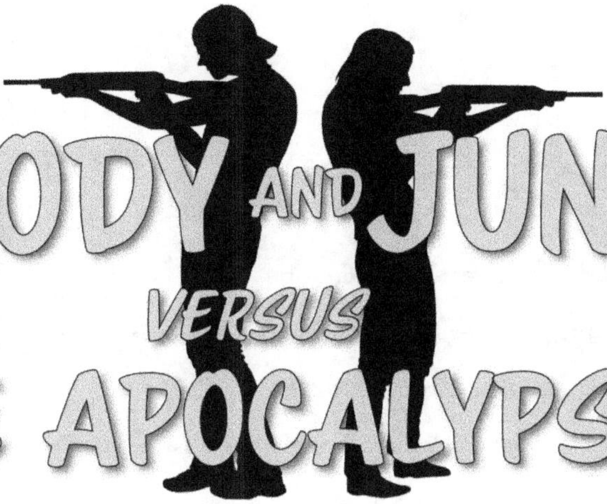

CHAPTER ONE

METEOR CRATER. It's exactly what it sounds like. A meteorite impact crater almost three quarters of a mile across, over five hundred feet deep, and roughly round. It looks pretty much like what you think—a crater on the moon but in the middle of the Arizona desert. The land here isn't grey like the moon but it is nearly as desolate, filled with chunks of whiteish limestone and covered with small tufts of dried grass with the green of spring just poking up here and there.

The edges of the crater mound up around the rim. It is the earth that was deposited here when the meteorite hit and exploded. The crater itself is a naked record of the geology and the history of this land.

It's not the Grand Canyon and it was a long time before it was proved that this was actually an impact crater. It was initially attributed to volcanic activity, and whatever you want to call it, it's a hell of a sight.

This area of Arizona is so barren it already felt moonish, but looking at the crater, the similarity is positively eerie. It's easy to imagine the Apollo astronauts testing out the first moon rover in the bottom of the crater.

And now, considering that we are the only ones here—except for the zombies we hear rumbling around in the visitor's center—it feels very much like the moon.

Survivors are out there, scattered in the remote land, broken into small squabbling tribes or even small extended families (let's face it, still some squabbling there too).

I used to be a go-it-alone survivor with nothing to lose. Until I met June Medina in Flagstaff and we picked up Dallas on our way out of the Grand Canyon escaping June's psychotic ex Talia.

"What are we doing here, Woody?" Dallas asks me. She is glancing nervously back at the visitor's center, a sprawling building perched on the edge of the crater made of brick with sandstone accents, all of it salmon-colored to blend into the terrain. The building is nestled among the pathways and platforms that thrust out over the edge.

Meteor Crater, surprisingly, is not a national monument. Not that that matters anymore, at all. It was privately owned, a little tourist trap. It was initially named Canyon Diablo Crater back in 1891 after the nearest town. That name certainly gives it a more sinister feel, one to go with the thump of the Zs on the picture window behind us.

June looks at me, all tough-as-hell and pixie beautiful with her blue eyes and light brown skin. We've been in this situation before. At the Desert View Overlook on the South Rim of the Grand Canyon. We stopped for the view and ended up fighting for our lives.

I adjust my Diamondback baseball cap and shrug. "We are taking a moment," I say. "Breathing. Recharging."

We escaped Talia and her minions in a race across the high desert east of Flagstaff that involved gunfire and Molotov cocktails and me getting shot in the arm. It was just a flesh wound and June had patched me up, but it hurt and I needed a moment. And the gunshot I had taken to the head a week ago ached and was starting to itch. It too was just a flesh wound thanks to June, but "to the head," you know. We were short on sleep, food, and water, and I just really needed a moment.

The sun is just coming up to the east, peeking up over the rim of the crater. The spring air is cold and the view is spectacular. Desert rolling away as far as the eye can see, slipping into the colorful swaths of the painted desert to the east and the San Francisco Peaks rising up to the west.

This is what you get with land this desolate. Views. Epic views. Like you can see forever.

"So Talia can catch up with us?" Dallas asks.

I turn away from the rising sun and face Dallas. She's in her early thirties, tall and curvy, with brown hair down to her shoulders. She has shorts on—it will get hot later—and a denim jacket which is not quite warm enough for a morning like this.

I kick at the cracked and debris-covered pathway. Things like this seem to degrade quickly without humans around. I draw my green army surplus jacket close and nod towards the view. "We are running. From Talia. I get that. She wants revenge for what happened down at Phantom Ranch. She wants June. She wants you and me dead."

I adjust my Diamondbacks baseball cap and shrug. "This is our life now. Looking for a home. Running from a psychotic, petty, wannabe warlord. But if there is not enough time to take a moment. To see the beauty around us. To have a second to think..." I shrug again, take June's hand, and watch the sun crawl up over the lip of the crater.

"And you're okay with this?" Dallas asks June.

June is the shortest of us and the toughest. She served in the Army. Can shoot like you wouldn't believe. And survived Talia after the world went to shit, faking her death by zombie just to get away. She smiles at Dallas. "Yeah. We are taking five minutes here. Chill, girl."

Dallas sighs and silence descends.

It's the silence of the apocalypse. Pervasive and deep. Complete. There is no road noise. No honking horns. No buzz of electricity. Just the slight hum of the breeze as it caresses the rocks and the grass. Far in the distance, the yip of coyotes breaks the silence. Only the banging on the window from the hungry Zs spoil the silence.

It is just a moment. That is all I am looking for. A moment of stillness and peace in the midst of the madness of survival. A moment that gives me hope. A moment that fills me with resolve.

The day will be a fight, that is guaranteed. And no longer being the go-it-alone survivor, I have things to fight for. June, whom I love, and Dallas, who despite the constant shit she gives me is my best friend. I love them both. They make this fight worth it. They make my life about something more than just survival, something more than just me.

"Thank you, Dallas," I say while I squeeze June's hand. We walk away from the crater and towards the day and the adventure that awaits.

CHAPTER TWO

ONE OF THE things I like best about the desert is its honesty. Snakes have fangs. Cacti have needles. The shape of the land and its dangers are visible for anyone to see.

Sure, it's deadly, but in an upfront way. You step on a cactus, it's going to hurt. You mess with a snake and you're going to get bit. You don't have supplies for the heat and the distance and you are going to die.

The desert doesn't hide what it is and that's what I like about it. Unlike people. Unlike psychotic, petty, wannabe warlords. Talia, June's ex, in particular.

Talia let June and I go at Phantom Ranch, only to send Dallas after us to slow us down. She also let Dallas and me go after June traded herself for our lives only to trap us in an unforgiving desert with almost no chance of survival.

But Talia is like the desert to me now. I don't trust a thing she says and know that we must be ready for her around every corner. Because she won't stop. She won't give up. And she is all needles and poison.

After our sunrise moment at Meteor Crater, we head to the parking lot and get to work. All three of us patrol it, weapons out. Me with my bat and the girls with their guns. We'd been here long enough that any Zs in the parking lot should have made themselves known, but you can't be too careful.

There are about twelve vehicles. First priority is gas, so with the girls guarding, I get to siphoning into our jerry cans, managing to not get a mouthful of gas this time.

We then do a quick round of scrounging. One in the vehicle and two guarding. Yes. We are paranoid. Talia is out there. Talia is coming for us.

Our "shopping" expedition, as Dallas likes to call it, is fairly successful. We find some food. Dallas gets herself a better jacket. I find a baseball bat which I take to serve as a backup, and Dallas finds something essential and turns it into a cringe-worthy moment.

"Here you go, lover boy," she says, coming out of small a RV, with her new pink down jacket, slapping a box of condoms in my hand.

I feel my cheeks burn. In retrospect, I know that she was jealous, that she wanted somebody too, but in that moment it wasn't fun.

I don't dare look at June and swallow hard.

"What's wrong?" she asks, a smile playing on her lips accentuating her noticeable smile lines. "You guys have been practicing safe sex, haven't you?"

I clear my throat, my jaw moving, but I don't come up with words.

"Or are you guys ready to restart the human race?" she continues with a laugh.

Because it is laughable. What would we do with a baby in this environment? And do I even want to bring a child into this world? Does June? My mind goes crazy for a moment trying to figure out diapers and doctors and formula and cribs and toys and wondering if we should be married first and who is going to marry us, but does June even want to get married, and isn't it way too soon in our relationship to even think about these things much less talk about them?

I glance at June and she's got her eyes on the horizon looking for danger, all business. Well, I can't imagine this conversation hasn't gotten to her too, but her back is to me and I can't tell.

"Just nod your head and say thank you, Diamondback," Dallas says.

I plaster a fake smile on my face, shove the condoms in my pocket, and say with as much sarcasm as possible, "Thank you, Lonestar. You really *are* my best friend."

She snorts. "Damn right!"

The rest of our "shopping expedition" is uneventful. We hear the distant bangs from the visitor's center. The Zs have locked onto us with their fresh-brains radar but there doesn't seem to be enough of them to break out. If they've been stuck in there for a year, they're probably very weak, like the Z June and I killed and dissected at the Grand Canyon.

When we're ready, I lay out a map of Arizona on the hood of our pickup truck. It doesn't look "new when the apocalypse happened" anymore. It's dusty, it has bullet holes in the tailgate, scratches in its beautiful black paint job, and the cab is a mess, looking like it's been occupied by homeless hoarders. But I love it all the more. Its damage means our survival.

I point to Meteor Crater on the map, south of I-40 and east of Flagstaff. "The fastest way, pre-apocalypse, would be to take I-40 east to Holbrook," I run my finger along the map, "and then head south through Show Low and then through Pinetop-Lakeside and over towards Greer. It's like 150 miles."

They are both staring at me, nodding. I'm the Arizona boy and the White Mountains was my bright idea, and the rule about no more unspoken plans is clear, so I am taking my time and laying it out.

"But there is Winslow, Joseph City, and Holbrook itself to deal with," I continue, looking pointedly at Dallas.

The morning is cool and she's encased in her new jacket. It's pink and down with white fur trim. She looks ridiculous and she looks warm. Any jacket in an apocalypse, I guess.

She bites her lip. "I was in Holbrook when Talia and company came through and 'recruited' me."

"How was it?" June asks. "What does this path look like?"

Our plan was to keep off the main roads, to keep to the dirt roads that roam across this land. We have enough gas and our odds of missing Talia go up. But it makes sense to understand the territory.

She shrugs and I am having trouble with the jacket. She looks like one of those pink snowball treats. It makes it hard to take her seriously, although I've seen her in action, and her skills extend beyond her biting sarcasm and wicked tongue.

"It shouldn't be bad," she says. "As long as the Zs have stayed where we put them. Talia's group, she called them Alpha Company then, had a routine where they would bait the Zs, lure them into a big old building or a fenced parking area, and trap them. As the new 'recruit,' I was the bait."

Her round face is puckered like she had just eaten something horrible. "The new recruits were always the bait. She went through them pretty fast." She plasters a fake smile on her face. "Good thing I can run."

"This happened in Holbrook and Winslow?" I ask.

She nods. "Yeah. First you bait and trap the Zs and then you go 'shopping.'" She shrugs like it wasn't a big deal, but the sour look on her face tells a different story.

"And we already decided we aren't going that way," I say. "She's probably waiting for us on I-40." I take a deep breath and point back to where we are. "We can either parallel I-40 on dirt roads or head south from here and get into the national forest sooner."

I run my finger south. "It will be slow going, probably with lots of wrong turns, but we'll try to make it down to Heber-Overgaard and then Show Low is not far to the east. No cities here before Show Low, only small communities. What do you guys think?"

We have a small democracy here. Three people means we always make a decision if it comes down to voting.

June furrows her brow and looks closely at the map. "There is no direct route, is there?"

I shake my head. "No. And we don't want to go as far south as Payson—too big, maybe fifteen thousand people."

I don't say it, but they can do the very simple math. Each one of these people could be Zs now.

"We'll have to find a way through on the dirt roads," I say.

June gestures towards the back of the truck and the supplies we inherited at the South Rim from the well-supplied group there that got taken out by the tourist zombie horde. "Any forest service maps back there?"

I nod and smile. "Yup. We didn't have time to dig them out before our last adventure."

"Well, then, let's get the hell out of here," Dallas says. She looks around warily as if she expects to see a line of trucks coming for us.

I dig the forest service maps out and we get moving.

ᛕᛉᚦ ᛉᚠ ᛉᚦᛉ

I'M NOT a human blessed with the illusion that I will live forever. Even before the Zs came, that wasn't one of my foibles. My grandmother died when I was a teenager. Cancer. My parents dragged me to Globe, Arizona to visit her. The living room of her double-wide had been cleared out so a narrow hospital bed could be put in. It smelled dank and dark, a little bit like the Zs smell, the kind of scent that makes your heart beat fast and sticks in your nose.

My father had been estranged from his mother and we hadn't seen her for three years. She seemed old to me then, but she really wasn't, somewhere in her late sixties. It was so tense, my father seeing his brother and sister for the first time in years. They had a hushed, tense conversation, but all I could look at was the frail old woman in the bed.

She had never been thin, but now she was and that just didn't seem right. Her cheeks sagged and she was too pale. Her short hair was a lot greyer than I remembered, only bits of brown left.

"Come here, boy," she said, her voice coming out as a croak. "Let me see you."

She had a twang in her voice, having been born in Alabama.

I didn't want to get closer to that smell or to her, but then she smiled and her pale blue eyes brightened. "Don't be afraid, Woody. I'm just dying. It's the most normal thing in the world."

"It is?" I asked, taking a step closer.

She nodded, the extra flesh at her neck wobbling in a way that made my stomach turn just a little bit. "It is. It's God's gift to us."

She said God with a capital "G." You could hear it in the way she talked. My family didn't go to church and if we said "god" in our house it most definitely had a lowercase "g."

She laughed. My face must have been comically scrunched up. "You don't believe me?" she asked, her hand coming out from under the sheet and the old brown blanket.

Her hand was smattered with age spots, had blue veins visible below the surface, and flesh hung off her upper arm loose and wobbly. But I took her hand and it was so warm and her skin was so soft. She tugged gently, I don't think she had more strength than that, and she pulled me close.

Her breath was dank and seemed to be the source of much of that zombielike rotting smell. I imagined that there were worms in her gut eating her from the inside out.

But she smiled and all those thoughts went away. I remembered her teaching me how to bake cookies and how sick I got after she let me eat as many as I liked. I remembered trips to Lake Roosevelt with her and my grandfather. I remembered how she would go crazy decorating for Christmas so not one single surface of her home was spared something bright and shiny.

"Death is not to be feared, Woody," she said. "Do I look afraid?"

I shook my head. "No, ma'am."

"But..." she prompted.

"I don't know if I believe in god," I said.

She laughed, it was phlegmy and it made the smell worse, but it was a happy sound. "Why, Woody, God does not need you to believe in Him. Believing is for you, not for Him."

I blinked, trying to process it. "But why do we have to die?" I asked.

"To make room," she said with a smile. I must have looked puzzled again because she continued. "Imagine this world if no one died. If the old stayed set in their ways and the young could not try new things. Imagine how crowded it would be and how very old fashioned."

"To make room," I said, echoing the words as I tried to understand them. What if my great-grandmother was here and my great-great-grandmother and my great-great-great-grandmother? And all their children and all their children's children. My eyes widened and I nodded. That would be terrible, with each previous generation more old fashioned than the last.

"But I will miss you," I said.

Her smile was different this time. It was tinged with sadness. "And I will miss you too, Woody." There were tears in her eyes. "Thank you so much for coming."

The spell lasted for a little longer, just Grandma and me while the adults talked in hushed tones, her warm hand in mine. We didn't talk about death or god (lowercase "g" or uppercase "G") but about some of the fun things we had done.

The smell bothered me less and I was so grateful that I had gotten to see her. Even with her skin sagging and her breath dark and dank.

When the tone of the adults talking changed, when it was clear the spell was about to be broken, I said, "I love you, Gran."

She smiled so wide her eyes narrowed in folds of old skin but the blue sparkled. "And I love you, my Woody man."

I didn't leave believing in god, but I did leave unafraid of death.

This world, right now, doesn't need me to die to make room for the next generation. There may not be a next generation. I have to wonder about my grandmother and her "to make room" reason for death. If there was a god, is this the plan? Have the Zs come to "make room"?

It aligns fairly nicely with June's thought that it is Gaia, the earth itself, that is the source of the infection, that she is thinning out the overgrown human population for the health of the planet.

Or my crazy thought that it's time travelers or aliens that created the virus for the same reason.

All of these are just thoughts, strange musings, my mind trying to grasp at a reason for what has happened to us all. Just trying to make sense of something that seems senseless.

But what counts now is survival. Of the ones I love. My family of choice. June and Dallas.

CHAPTER THREE

THE DESERT here is tinged with reddish earth. I know it's iron in the soil, but the land has sweeps of the color like a giant with a paintbrush wanted to add variety to the simple desert. The white chunks of limestone that were so prevalent around the crater are not here. It makes me think that the meteor blasted through a thick layer of it when it came crashing down fifty thousand years ago.

I stop the truck as it points south, leaving the paved road that goes to Meteor Crater onto one of the many dirt roads back here. It's desolate, lonely land with scattered grass, mostly dried, some new green shoots, and low weedy bushes newly green from spring rains.

To our left rises up the low hump of the crater's rim and mesas squat on the distant horizon as the dirt road cuts through the gentle rolls of the land.

The windows are rolled down and I can smell the dry dirt. I am hesitating, and I don't know why.

"I've got the road spotted on the map," June says from the passenger's seat, the forest service map lying on her lap and draped on the dash, crinkling when she points at it. "I know how to get us down to state road 87. We'll have to be on it for a few miles, but it should be fine, not much in the area."

I nod but don't start us down the road. Something isn't right. It's too quiet. It's too peaceful. Maybe I've been running too long. Maybe the string of close calls has left me uncomfortable with something going right.

And then it hits me. We've been so focused on ourselves but we are not the only survivors out here. "What's going to happen to Phantom Company?" I ask, turning to Dallas who's in the backseat.

She's still got on her pink down jacket. Her mouth opens and I'm sure she's going to deliver a sharp retort, but then her brown eyes widen and she pushes her brown hair back behind an ear.

"Shit," she says, biting her lip.

"Talia," June says.

I nod and look forward towards our escape. To a fighting chance to get to the White Mountains and get away from Talia. To being with those that I care about the most. To a future that might actually be peaceful.

"So Talia took out Brown," Dallas begins, "the Flagstaff psycho-prissy-whatever-you-call-them and took his gang over. This is after Harris, the second in command of Phantom Company, betrayed her during your insane dynamite laden rescue of June."

"She'll want revenge," June says quietly.

Dallas snorts. "She'll want the territory and the people."

"She's after us now..." I begin.

"But will be going there next," Dallas finishes.

"And she'll kill anyone there that opposes her," June adds. "Harris and the rest of them that were there during that confrontation."

"There are some good people there," Dallas says. "I mean, I hated it—God, so much—but they've got food and shelter and the goddamn Colorado River for water. They've got a good thing going."

"Talia won't be satisfied with Phantom Ranch anymore," June says. "She'll use the people and the resources there to take over more territory."

It's a barrage of information from the two of them, each fact pounding into me. Each truth painful. June is silent for a long time. We all are. And then Dallas says, so quietly that we can barely hear her, "If it weren't for Talia, Phantom Ranch would have been goddamn Shangri-La."

She's right. Warm enough to have a long growing season. All the water you can possibly use. Deer and other game in the area. Isolated, there weren't any Zs there until June and I led the tourist zombie horde down.

"Better than the White Mountains," I mumble.

I'm still staring down the road, the bits of spring grass, the red-tinged earth, the distant mesas, but I feel their gazes on me. I shut the engine off and get out of the truck and start pacing on the dirt road. They follow. It's still cool and it feels good to be moving.

"Better?" June asks. I don't blame her. I pitched the White Mountains hard. I made a big deal about it. Because I think it would be a good place to go and because I needed something for us all to fight for. A goal to keep us motivated.

I nod. "The bottom of the canyon is warmer. No harsh winters. Good growing season. Plenty of deer. Hot in the summer, but that's survivable."

June stops walking and stares at me while I pace. Dallas has her arms wrapped around herself despite the pink coat and is chewing on her lip.

Talia hasn't found us yet. We aren't that far off the highway, so however she deployed her resources it didn't extend here. We can be done with her. Now. Today.

But Talia is fixing to go from being a psychotic, petty, wannabe warlord to a Warlord. With a capital "W" and no longer wannabe. She's still going to be psychotic and petty, but that kinda goes without saying.

Is this what the world will become now? Nut jobs like Talia grabbing power because they are brutal enough and psychotic enough? We can hide from it, I know we can, for a while at least.

I turn back and look at June and Dallas and can see it in their eyes. They have come to the same conclusion.

Both June and Dallas still have bruises on their faces from our last face-to-face encounter with Talia, splotches of fading purple that is yellow on the edges. My wound to my head where she tried to put a bullet in my brain is scabbed up and itchy. My arm where one of her goons just shot me hurts like hell.

We survived Talia, but barely.

I'm still and we are all just staring at each other. I don't think anyone wants to speak about this further and make it more real.

"How... how could we help?" June finally asks, her voice quiet, her blue eyes drilling into me. Dallas is staring at me too.

I shrug. "The way we snuck up on them, down at Phantom Ranch... easy to protect against. Motion sensors wired to a radio transmitter attached to solar chargers. We could use the dynamite and rig both bridges to explode. Regular drone flights from up above Phantom Ranch with lookouts 24-7. Escape routes in case they come down the river on rafts and we can't take them out quick enough. Scouts on the rim with solar-powered CB radios so we know when someone is coming.

"Phantom Ranch is remote and defensible, but not like it is now."

"And that means we have to get back to Phantom Ranch," Dallas says quietly.

June nods. "Past Talia and all the people she has looking for us."

Silence descends, just the breeze hissing over the desert. No highway noise. No airplanes. True silence.

But my mind is not silent. The odds of us getting back to Phantom Ranch are complete shit. And then we don't know what kind of reception we would get. And then we would have to contend with the full force of Talia and her new band of nut jobs.

"Well," Dallas begins loudly, "what the hell kind of life expectancy do we have anyway?"

And she's right. It's not good. Zombies. Disease. Psychotic, petty, wannabe warlords trying to become real Warlords.

"Who the hell wants to live forever?" June adds with a casual shrug. But I can see it on her face. She's scared. I think Talia is the only thing in this world that scares that woman.

And they're both staring at me, the silence thickening again.

"I'm in," I say, trying to make it sound casual. "Wherever you guys go, I go."

"You hear that, you bitch," Dallas yells, swiveling so she's facing north. "We are coming for you! We are going to turn Phantom Ranch against you. And then we are going to beat your skinny ass!"

We all laugh, nice and early in the day too for my second goal of each day of the apocalypse. But it's a strained laughter, all released tension and not amusement. I stop laughing first because I have an inkling in my mind, a tiny voice that tells me that we are going to have to kill Talia to stop her. That we best do it here before she takes her forces and marches after us to Phantom Ranch. And that it's going to have to be me that kills her. She used to be June's partner, and Dallas hates her too much and is way too unpredictable.

"Well, let's figure out a new plan," I say, striding towards the truck and not saying a word about what I just realized.

CHAPTER FOUR

IN THE END we decide on Leupp. Where we saw the lights from Wupatki National Monument and the 40s. Despite my fantasy about how the Navajo and Hopi must have it all together and they don't need some white man barging in, we have to have another way around Flagstaff, and the rez is the only choice.

Talia is in control of East Flagstaff and the 40s and it would be foolish to head back the way we came. The reservation is different territory, unknown, but we have to take our chances.

And that means we have to head north, parallel I-40 back to the west slightly, cross the highway past the ruins of Two Guns, and head towards the ghost town of Canyon Diablo. Yes, the one Meteor Crater was originally named after.

I've never been there, but it's the most direct way onto the rez.

But we have preparations to make. I send the drone up to look for movement—and yes, with it being light out, this is a risk—while Dallas and June do surgery on the truck.

I'm not happy about it, but the chase through the 40s made it clear that we need to be able to move from the cab into the bed unencumbered. And that means pulling out the rear window.

I can't watch. I'm on a rock down the road a bit focused on the drone controls, a small tablet hooked up for the camera. I fly it low and to the east for a few minutes so it's not a dead giveaway of our location if someone spots it, and I get some good aerial views of Meteor Crater.

I move the drone up in the air slowly taking it a few thousand feet up, no more height regulations now. We are about five miles south of the highway. The red earth extends to the north, the land relatively level but generally sloping down as you go farther east away from the San Francisco Peaks.

There's not much to see. The blacktop of the road to Meteor Crater goes fairly straight to the north. I can just make out the east-west cut of I-40, and to the west the zigzagging path of Canyon Diablo is visible.

It is beautiful land. Desolate land. But I'm not here for the view. Everything is still as far as I can see.

I take the drone slowly down, and when it's only a few hundred feet up I let it drop rapidly into the crater. My old man and I hiked it when I was about six. My brother was too young for such an adventure (and really, I was too) and I loved having my father to myself. It was hot as hell and we didn't have enough water and the heat was unbearable.

But we got to see the assemblage of junk on the bottom. A fenced off area that was part of an old mine and some old rusted equipment. This was where the Apollo astronauts practiced with the moon rover.

We were the only dummies hiking that day and I remember hiding under a rocky overhang on the steepest part of the accent not thinking I could take another step. My face was burning red and I was a little dizzy, my mouth so dry. My father was red too and we panted for the longest time, sweat dripping off us.

"Always up for a good adventure, aren't you, Woody?" he asked. I didn't inherit my freckles from my old man and his hair was a darker brown than mine, but he had the kindest face, always with a ready smile.

I nodded my head vigorously despite the dizziness. "Yes, sir. What's our next adventure, Dad?"

My father smiled, his best feature really, and I felt like I could do the hike all over again. He laughed and we sat there chatting until we were cool enough to finish the climb.

It was a good day. Most days with my father out on the land were good days.

I take another moment, enjoying flying the drone out of the crater, zooming up above the rim with ease. My father is one of the things about the pre-apocalyptic world that I miss the most.

I pack up the drone and turn back and see that June and Dallas have done their part. The truck no longer has a back window. Maybe we need to find some steel plates and weld them on and turn it into the kind of vehicle in the Mad Max movies. This isn't Australia, but the land has a similar look and the problems are also similar too.

"Anything out there?" June asks.

I shrug. "Not that I could see. We should stop at the RV park by the highway and do some reconnaissance before we get on a dirt road and start kicking up dust."

⚰ 🧍 🧍

FIVE MILES to the RV park.

Five miles to the highway.

Ten minutes going slow, watching close, keeping our eyes on the horizon, looking for signs of movement.

A couple more minutes as we start doing a quick pass through the RV park. We didn't stop on our way in and we could use more gas.

And then it all goes to shit.

The RV park is verdant compared to the rest of the land, with tall trees, a mix of evergreen and deciduous throwing shade for the campers that used to stay here. It's fronted by a gas station, but we started back here for the more rounded "shopping" experience.

It doesn't take long to find it. We are all out on foot doing our initial sweep and there is a stack of milk crates set up in the middle of the RV park. On it sits a box with a hastily wrapped red ribbon around it. Written on the side with a sharpie it says "For Woody and June and Dallas. Open now and let the fun begin." There's a little heart drawn above "June."

"Shit!" I say.

"Damn," June says.

Dallas brings it home with a string of curses that is both creative and blistering.

It's Talia, none of us need to say anything. We were still for too long. We really hadn't gotten away.

I take a deep breath, trying to get my brain in gear. Talia knew where we were and could have attacked at any time. She knew we would take a pass through the RV park on our way out, any survivor would have, really. Whatever this is, it's not the end of us, it's the beginning of the game she wants to play, of the revenge she wants to extract.

I take a step forward, but June catches my arm. "It's okay," I say with a smile, though my heart is beating a mile a minute. "If she wanted us dead, we would be dead by now."

But I am careful. I don't open the top of the box and I don't move it either. I pull the knife from my belt and cut open the side, the noise of the knife sawing through the cardboard garish and loud.

Inside is a military walkie-talkie.

Underneath it is a note:

There are three rules to this game:

1. *I win.*
2. *The more you play, the longer you survive.*
3. *I win.*

So let's talk.

The box is otherwise empty and I just stand there holding the walkie-talkie, staring at it.

"Shit," June says again and I look at her. She's staring up. I follow her gaze and high above us is a drone, the same model of quadcopter I was just flying is hovering above us.

"The bitch is stealing your tricks," Dallas says, looking around the RV park. There are maybe eight RVs here and no sign of Zs, but suddenly it all looks a whole lot more sinister.

Back at the 40s she had a man that had cobbled together radio trackers they attached to the zombies they released to track us, and now the quadcopter above us.

I was no longer the only one using tech intelligently.

I look back over the note. "The more you play, the longer you survive... So let's talk."

She knows we are here. She knows we have the walkie-talkie. She wants us to initiate the conversation. So I press the button. "So what happens if we don't play?" I say, keeping my voice as calm as possible.

"Then you die," Talia replies. It's her. I'd recognize the smugness in that voice anywhere and her gentle southern accent is unmistakable.

I'm about to reply when the RV a few spots down explodes.

Well... it's not really like that, my mind has to assemble it all together. First, there's the flash of light, then the deafening sound, and then the wall of hot air hits us, followed by debris raining down on us.

It wasn't a huge explosion, it wasn't meant to hurt us, but it sure gets our attention. By the time my mind puts it all together, I'm down on the cement and June and Dallas are too.

I traded some real dynamite for June down at the Phantom Ranch. Talia clearly took that with her when she left. It makes me wonder if Harris, who helped us get away when she wouldn't keep her bargain, is still alive. Maybe she already had Phantom Ranch back under her control.

There's laughter coming from the walkie-talkie. I dropped it and it's lying on the cement a few feet away. I reach for it, but Dallas gets to it before me.

"Just show yourself, you little bitch," Dallas spits into the walkie. "I don't need a gun. I don't need a knife. I'll tear you apart with my bare hands. I'll—"

"Oh, Dallas-girl," Talia says, cutting her off, "you were always more bark than bite, but I like the spunk. Makes me think you all will make a good run of this."

Dallas is on her knees and she reaches up with the walkie-talkie. It's clear she's going to smash it on the cement. I surge up to stop her, but June beats me to it and pulls it out of Dallas's hand.

She stares at it, her blue eyes wide and her beautiful round face contorted into an ugly mask. Her feelings have to be the most complicated of us all.

With what is clearly a great effort, she wrests control of her emotions, her jaw locking, and hands the walkie-talkie to me. "You have to be the one to talk to her," she says.

I nod. I want to take her in my arms, to hold her, but now is so not the time. I take a deep breath. "So we've had a little discussion, Talia," I begin, "and we'd all like to hear about this lovely game you've got planned for us. The days are really too long and we all are looking forward to something fun and different to do."

The chuckling that begins her reply is nothing short of evil. And insane. "You know, Mr. Woody Woodpecker, you are the one I underestimated. I will not do that again."

I look at June and Dallas but neither of them will meet my eyes. Dallas is still on her knees and June is hugging herself and looking away.

"Right back at ya, Talia," I reply.

Because I did underestimate her. Horribly. We should have never stopped moving. I should have known she would up her game.

She snorts her reply as if she can't believe anyone ever underestimated her and how foolish that person must be. Talia is a raging narcissist. It is the only possible reaction she can have. I must keep this in mind.

"Before you start worrying your pretty little heads about such things," she begins, "I will tell you that we did not sneak in last night and booby trap your truck, that the only eyes I have on you right now is the drone, that I will never lie to you during our little game, and you are free to make whatever choices you want."

We're all now thinking that the truck is booby trapped, that everything she's telling us will be a lie, and that she has sharp shooters on us right now, although with the land as flat as it is that's not really possible.

"Thank you for that," I reply, because she clearly wants a reply.

"But—and this *is* the fun part—there are booby traps on your course, and your choices have consequences," she says.

"Why don't we just settle this, Talia," I say. I've got my back to June and Dallas. We don't have time to plan this together and I don't want to see their reactions. "Just you and me. Bare hands. No rules. You are clearly stronger and better trained than I am."

"Your misogynistic pseudo-gallantry makes me sick," she says, her voice communicating the sneer that must be on her face. "The game is set. I make the rules. I—"

"I am sorry to hear you are afraid of a fair fight," I say evenly, cutting her off.

"I am afraid of nothing!" she shouts. "Certainly not the famous 'Diamondback.'" She must have learned about my nickname from the former East Flagstaff psychotic, petty, wannabe warlord.

"So then we have a deal?" I ask.

June moves herself into my field of view and she's shaking her head rapidly. "No," she hisses.

"Are you sayin' you don't want to play my game?" she asks, her voice suddenly calm.

June points to the RV that exploded and grabs my arm and pulls me towards the trees in the center of the park. Talia's note says, "The more you play, the longer you survive."

All the RVs could be rigged to explode.

"No," I say. "Just trying to understand the scope of your game. Of course we want to play."

"Good," she says, her voice actually sounding happy like she's a little girl and we just agreed to play jump rope with her. "We're going to test your knowledge of Arizona now, Mr. Woodpecker. Go to where the Apache died and you will find direction. You have fifteen minutes to succeed or the game is over."

CHAPTER FIVE

I'M an Arizona boy through and through. While I was born and raised in Phoenix, I spent a lot of time roaming the state with my father. Also, an Arizona boy. He was proud of his state and he knew it well. It was the kind of thing he liked to share with his sons.

So we had been to Meteor Crater when I was six and then poked through the ruins of Two Guns afterwards. I knew the history, how in the late 1800s the Apache had used Canyon Diablo as a hiding place to raid Navajo settlements. I knew that the Navajo found them, threw burning sagebrush into the cave they were hiding in, and shot any Apache trying to escape, killing forty-two of them.

Not surprising this was the location of Talia's first clue in her "game." It was a place of terrible violence.

I vaguely remember the cave and my father telling me the grim story under the hot sun. "They call this the Apache Death Cave, son," he had started solemnly. He did love Arizona, but he didn't hide from its darker side either.

I was six and antsy and uncomfortable but he insisted that we be there, in view of the cave, to tell me the story. My grasp of time was imprecise and I kept expecting an Apache Indian to come running out and I kept looking around for one of the Navajos to come with their burning sagebrush. The place ended up just freaking me out. But that was about twenty years ago and we have fifteen minutes to find it.

I had asked Talia for a one-on-one showdown and that was what she already had planned. She said she made the mistake of underestimating me and now she is testing me.

More than that, it's clear she is trying to break me. Push me past my limits. Turn me into someone that June doesn't trust, that June doesn't want to be with.

Because this is all about June and Talia's obsession with her. And I'm the person who took Talia's place in June's life, so she means to hurt me. Badly.

In the RV park, we don't talk. We run to the truck and jump in. We tear out of the park, past the gas station and onto Old Route 66. Even before the zombies, this part of Route 66 was just a dirt road. Then it was a decent dirt road, now it's a post-apocalyptic dirt road. And that means debris and erosion, but no washboarding. Not enough traffic for that.

The road is a straight shot for about three miles when it hits the Two Guns exit on I-40 and dips down to the south.

How do I explain Two Guns, Arizona?

Well, before the apocalypse, it looked like the apocalypse happened fifty years ago with the rocky ruins of the faux western town that had been built on this site in the twenties, and the husks of the more modern buildings constructed in the sixties. At various points there had been small zoos, restaurants, and several different gas stations. All of it close to the snaking rim of Canyon Diablo.

Up front is a newer relic, a just-off-the interstate gas station and garage from the sixties. It's just the graffiti-covered walls now and it has a three-bay garage connected to a small convenience store. Back then you could get gas and get your car worked on. Near it is a wooden shack of some sort, the shingles long gone as it lists to one side. Probably used to be a small trading post. Next to it is the barely readable "2 Guns" sign, the black paint badly faded and covered in fading graffiti.

Up behind it, on a hill, is the husk of an old KOA with the signature A-frame store.

These are the new parts of Two Guns.

The older parts, the zoo and the gas station that was on Route 66, as well as the old bridge over Canyon Diablo, are just to the west, closer to the canyon. These were built back in the late 1920s.

They are literal ruins, the pale Kaibab limestone the walls were built out of most of what remains, the majority of the wood having rotted away long ago.

All of this is built on this limestone-littered, desolate land, the ground covered in dry grass with spring green growing up in the middle, sagebrush, and the occasional scraggly bush.

We speed past the new relics and I stop us in front of the first set of limestone ruins, a couple of walls with "MOUNTAIN LIONS" painted along the top of the wall in fading black paint.

It's strange, but looking at them, they are not that much different than the much older ruins at Wupatki. Well, the stone is paler and not as carefully built, the rocks larger and not fitting together as well, but it reminds me of that. Rock stays long after man is gone. There is something more noble about this effort than the more modern ruins we just passed.

Maybe it's that these will look pretty much the same in another century. Maybe it's that they blend in with the land, made of rock found in the area, and don't stick out as much as the more modern human constructs do.

We get out of the truck and I look around. It hasn't changed in twenty years, but I have.

"Ten minutes, kiddies," Talia says on the walkie-talkie. "Go to where the Apache died, and you will find direction."

"Well?" Dallas says, staring at me.

The ruins of Two Guns extend from where we are along the canyon as it snakes to the west. We have to find a cave. I can see the

Old Route 66 bridge below us and I start jogging toward it. I know that Apache Death Cave is on the canyon and that will give us a view.

The Old Route 66 Canyon Diablo bridge is a one-lane affair situated on a narrow and straighter portion of the canyon. Below is a dry wash but with actual bushes and green growing things, taking advantage of the relative concentration of water in the desert.

To our right, the canyon curves towards I-40 and the current bridge. To the left it twists arounds almost 180 degrees below that first set of ruins.

The air is still cool but the sun is hot.

"What are we looking for?" June asks.

"A cave along the canyon," I say. "There was a ruin next to it and..." I am struggling to pull the old memories out. "I remember my father pointing to the ruins of a store that was built next to it. He told me that they used to give tours of the cave and they sold the skulls of the murdered Apaches in the store."

They're both staring at me. And I get it. Yeah, this was almost a hundred years ago, but the callousness of it is shocking. Even in the post-apocalyptic world we are living in.

But we don't have a discussion. June points to the east where the canyon makes its sharp turn and a jumble of ruins dangle on the edge.

I stare, hesitating. It doesn't look right, but I don't know if I ever saw it from this angle. I scan the canyon again and then nod. "That must be it."

"Are you sure?" Dallas asks.

"No," I say "I haven't been here since I was six." It comes out more defensive than I would have liked.

She opens her mouth to retort, but the walkie-talkie comes to life. "Five minutes, kiddies," Talia says.

CHAPTER SIX

THE RUIN IS A GOOD ONE, all four limestone walls intact, a narrow door, even some pieces of wood in the ceiling. It's small by today's standards, but a century ago things weren't built so big. It's made out of the same Kaibab limestone that Canyon Diablo cuts through, a pale off-white color.

This was the rustic store where tourists came in the late 1920s. I can imagine the tour guide taking his wide-eyed customers out of the cool of the stone building into the heat of the desert. "Just this way ladies and gentlemen, and you will see precisely why some say Two Guns is cursed. Why some have claimed to hear the screams of the Apache echoing across the decades from the caves just below us in the infamous—and rightly named, I might add—Canyon Diablo."

There is a crease in the canyon where it makes that sharp turn. There are jumbled limestone rocks and a decaying footbridge of some sort that is nothing more than a couple of long logs that look like telephone poles with rotting planking across it.

We ran here along the edge of the canyon and this is it. My twenty-year-old memory lights up. I remember the scramble down. This mini side-canyon is edged in sagebrush as is much of the rim of the canyon. The fuel that was used in this brutal act of revenge.

I scramble down with June and Dallas right behind me. It's all a tumble of limestone rocks and a quick corkscrew twist and we are clearly at the narrow entrance to the cave. Cooler air is rushing out to greet us, and along with it, the unmistakable growl of a zombie and some kind of distant clinking I can't quite place. I hear a buzzing sound and look up and see a drone watching us.

"Should I shoot it?" Dallas asks, just behind me. "Please. I really want to shoot it."

"Shut up, Dallas," June snaps.

June and I stare into the cave, a narrow crack that leads back into the earth. The sound of the Z echoing out. It must be back there a little ways.

"Time?" I ask.

"Three minutes," June says, glancing at her watch.

We don't have time to be careful. We don't have time to plan. We don't even have time to talk about it. This is not the way you do the apocalypse. You don't rush into anything without a plan.

"You don't have enough time, children," Talia says over the walkie, as if she had read my mind, the drone hovering closer like some annoying avatar for Talia. "Wasted time at the bridge. Tell you what. You all put your guns down before you go into the cave and I'll give you five more minutes."

We stare at each other and then at the dark entrance to the cave. This is a trap. It has to be. But Talia's goal here is not to kill us... well, not *just* to kill us.

I catch June's ocean-blue eyes and I can see from the worry on her face that she's come to the same conclusion. This isn't good, whatever it is that's about to happen, but there must be a chance of survival or Talia's little "game" will be over.

She nods, almost imperceptibly, pulls the gun from her hip and sets it down. "Deal," I say into the walkie and put it down. It won't work in there anyway. I grip my baseball bat in both hands and plunge in first with June right behind me.

"I... I have a bad feeling about this," Dallas says from behind us.

"Then guard the entrance," I snap without looking back. There's just no time.

Talia has not specified what happens if we stop playing the game, if we don't find "direction" here in the seven or eight minutes we now have left. But I suspect it involves a lot of people and a lot of guns and Dallas's and my deaths and June's capture.

In retrospect, this is what Talia wanted. She wanted us to rush. She didn't want us to think.

I duck under some old metal that was put up as lintel to keep the entrance from collapsing. It's tagged with graffiti and I have no idea what era it comes from.

The cave is narrow, maybe four feet wide as it zags back underneath the earth and I'm glad I still have my army surplus jacket on. The cave has remnants of crudely built walls made of limestone, maybe something the Apache built when they were doing their raids.

I still hear the growl of Zs, it's gotten a bit louder and it's clear now that there is more than one. The clinking sounds like a chain. As the darkness descends, I pull a flashlight from my belt, click it on, and stick it in my mouth. June pulls her flashlight.

"What are we looking for?" she whispers.

I shrug but keep moving. "Talia said to come here and we would 'find direction.'"

But there's nothing here but dirt and damp air and the smell of rotting flesh.

About ten yards in, there is light coming in from above and a wall on our left with a low entryway, like the kind you see in Wupatki. In fact, the construction of the wall and the one earlier is exactly like Wupatki and much neater than the buildings up above, the stones carefully chosen and fit together like a jigsaw puzzle. My first impression was wrong. The walls may be crude in technique, but skill was at work. The sound of the Zs is coming from that direction. The cave had been divided.

There's enough light that we don't need the flashlight, but I keep mine in my mouth and move forward quickly. I figure what we need is in with the Zs, but I don't want to go that way unless I have to. We bought ourselves the time, might as well use it.

We go up over a jumble of rocks and then I take another step forward and feel a slight resistance, hear a sharp clinking sound, and suddenly the Zs are getting louder.

"Shit!" I say.

"What?" June asks.

"Trip wire," I say, shining the flashlight and seeing a thin wire snaking back along the passageway. "Talia promised us booby traps."

The Zs get louder, their snarling quickening as they move towards their prey. That would be us.

We surge forward, the crack above us closes, it gets dark again, and the cave quickly opens up. It's a little over six feet tall. The forty-two Apache from the story would be a tight fit, but they could manage.

On the ceiling I can see some flat metal hooks that had been driven into the rock, probably where they hung lights from in the twenties when they brought tourists down here for a quick and safe little scare. I swing my head around, shining the light. There's nothing else in here but another narrow passage farther back.

I stick my head in and see it's another chamber, but low, not a good place to fight.

"Shit," June says, pulling her knife from her belt. No guns. Zs. Close quarters. This isn't going to be pretty.

And then three things happen at once.

There's shouting and cursing, the latter clearly Dallas, but there are other voices in the mix, male voices.

Burning branches start falling from the high cracks of the passageway we had just passed through.

And three zombies come into view.

But they aren't your normal zombies. They are wearing football helmets, and I recognize the lead zombie. Actually, all three of them look familiar.

As the smoke hits my nose, my stomach falls. Talia has trapped us in here with zombies, ones that have their heads protected, and is recreating what happened to the Apache when the Navajo got their revenge.

And this is Talia's revenge.

The first Z is short and stocky, over forty with a bland face, the nose recently broken with crusted blood on his mouth and a swollen cheek. He doesn't look much like a Z except for the whites of his eyes have gone yellow and the gut wound visible through his dirty white T-shirt that must have been what killed him. The T-shirt has some writing on it, but in the poor lighting I don't get a good look. He's got a metal collar around his neck with a chain dangling behind him.

This zombie was named Brown. Before I learned his name, I thought of him as Mr. Short and Stocky. He's the guy that captured us on the top of Mount Elden on the first full day of Woody and June versus the Apocalypse. The one I had to face again with Dallas when we were rushing back to the canyon to rescue June from Talia.

He led the gang that Talia just took over. And this is how she disposes of him.

He's flanked by two of his former lieutenants, big beefy boys, one of which June punched in the nose on our first full day together. They all have the same gut wound.

Now, Zs are hard to manage, what with them wanting to eat you, so getting Zs down here and chaining them up would be very, very hard. But that's not what they did. They dragged them down here alive, chained them up, and then killed them.

Just so we could face off with them.

Talia is sending a message. This is what happens to her enemies. This is what she plans for Dallas and me. And what makes it bad is this is definitely not as bad as what June has in store if Talia keeps her alive.

Smoke starts billowing up behind them and June and I both back up a step. No guns. My bat won't be of much use.

And this is just the first round of Talia's "game."

CHAPTER SEVEN

I WANT to tell June that I love her. I want to meet what looks like our imminent end with her knowing how much she means to me. I want to be the romantic and celebrate our brief love in this insane world up until the very last moment.

I am a realist. There will be a last moment. Even before the apocalypse there was always a last moment. Basic biology. It's the inevitable end that makes the moments you do have so precious.

And it occurs to me as my mouth opens to say those things, that there is a better way to express my love. By living through this madness.

Not to mention the smoke stinging my eyes and filling my nose will make it very hard to say anything. Flaming branches of sagebrush are still dropping down the crack in the passageway up ahead, and despite the cool of the cave, I am sweating like it's a summer day.

So instead of saying, "I love you, June Medina," I say, "They can't bite us, go for the knees."

Talia put football helmets on them with the guards still on. And they are brand new zombies, the fungus hasn't had a chance to take complete hold. That is overridden a bit by the brand-new-zombie voraciousness, but they aren't that coordinated.

June flashes me a wry smile and we back up farther into the cave so we can provide two different targets and split them up.

I can feel the smoke starting to catch in my lungs. We have to do this fast.

Brown heads towards me and the two beefy boys head towards June. Five hundred pounds worth of fresh Zs heading towards the love of my life and I... I let them. I do. June is way better trained at hand-to-hand combat than I am, being in the Army and all. And being June.

Brown lunges for me. I sidestep to the left, swing my bat, and am rewarded with the sharp crack of his kneecap breaking. He's still standing, somehow, trying to move towards me by hopping on one foot. If I had a moment, if the smoke wasn't thickening and my eyes weren't stinging, I would laugh.

The former psychotic, petty, wannabe warlord reduced to being a football-helmeted hopping Z. I think of trying to rip his helmet off to expose his head, but they even did the chin straps.

So I dance in and take out his other knee and he goes down.

Even as brand-new Zs they stink. Not the fungal funk that will come soon, but the cloying scent of rotting flesh mixing with the choking smell of smoke.

June is farther back in the cave, one of the beefy boys down and crawling toward her, the other backing her into the passageway that leads to that other, shorter cavern. And this is smart. She's small. She'll be way more maneuverable in there than the Z will.

But there's no time.

I rush up behind him and swing hard. My aim is off, the blow landing high, but his right femur snaps and he goes down.

"We got to get out of here," I say, coughing. The smoke is getting thick.

"Dallas," she says between coughs and nodding. "But what about our direction?"

The beefy Z grasps at June's leg and she stomps down on his arm with her hiking boots and I hear more bones snap.

My brain slips, like a bad clutch. I know the clue is here. I think I even saw it. I look down at the Z now grasping at June with its other hand and he's wearing a dark olive army surplus jacket like mine. So is the other beefy boy. But Brown was wearing a cheesy T-shirt that had writing on it.

"Brown," I say, coughing so much I'm finding it hard to speak. "T-shirt."

We move towards the Z that used to be Brown. He is crawling towards us. But he's on his stomach and I can't see his shirt. I avoid his grasping hands and stomp down on his neck, and while I hear bones cracking, it doesn't stop him. June stomps his hands and the hands of the other Z. They are still moving, but they are mostly harmless now. It's the smoke that's going to kill us.

I roll him over, and while I can see the cheesy red letters, my eyes are tearing so much I can't read it. It's three words. The first word starts with a "T" and the last word starts with an "E."

Zombie Brown is pawing at me with his ruined hands and I can't focus. I put the bat down, draw my knife from my belt and shove it through his eye, and he finally stops moving.

While I do that, June continues to stomp on the other two Zs crawling towards us.

I'm coughing nonstop and still can't make out the letters.

I use my knife to cut through the collar of the shirt and rip the damn thing off of him. It comes off in pieces, but it's something.

I can't talk anymore. We are both coughing too much. I'm starting to feel dizzy. I pick up my bat and grab her hand and we move out of the cave into the passageway. The smoke is thicker, there are burning branches all around, but we ignore them and run. Well, we try to run, but we are running out of oxygen. It's more a fumbling stumble where first I keep June from falling and then she keeps me from falling.

We get past the burning sagebrush and stumble through the cave, through the dark section until we can see the light of the entranceway, the steep jumble of limestone rocks, my tears making the shapes all melt together like some impressionistic painting.

The air is fresher here and we pause. We cough. We suck in oxygen. We try to stop the world from spinning. We don't see Dallas. Or anyone else.

We crawl out into the bright light and the walkie-talkie comes to life. It's Talia, her voice positively gleeful. "Dallas stopped playing the game," she says. "So, Dallas is now part of the game. You have one hour to follow your direction and save her."

CHAPTER EIGHT

TALIA SAID "DIRECTION" not "directions." We must follow our "direction."

It's a silly distinction, but that's what my brain focuses on as I cough, as we climb up the steep tumble of limestone out of the Apache Death Cave. Which almost became the Woody and June Death Cave.

The air is still cool and rich with oxygen. And I suck a deep breath in and am rewarded with more coughing. We are in no shape to follow our "direction," whatever the hell that is. We need time to recover. We need water and rest.

"Shirt," June gasps when we get to the top in front of the ruins of the old store and are sitting on the cool ground looking down towards the cave entrance, smoke puffing out.

Talia probably had people hidden in the old store. She kept us on a timeline so we couldn't be smart. So we couldn't do the things we know to do. The things you have to do to survive.

I fish in the pocket of my army surplus jacket and pull the remnants of the T-shirt out. The one zombie Brown was wearing. It didn't come away clean, I got some of it, and while my eyes are still watering, I can at least make out the red letters.

"e it Easy."

Part of the first word is missing.

"What the hell?" June says between coughs.

I shake my head trying to clear it. The T-shirt is super thin, really cheap. The kind of junk you would get in a cheesy tourist trap on the sale rack. The font is also tacky, with a rounded serif font that is trying to make it look cheerful. Whoever created this T-shirt didn't work very hard.

And how can this be "direction"?

"Dallas," June coughs, as if I need a reminder as to what the stakes are.

I had seen more in the cave, by the light of the little flashlight I had gripped in my mouth. It started with a... Damn it. I can't remember.

"I... I have to go back in," I mumble, moving to lever myself up.

"No," June says gently, taking my arm. Her grip is strong. "Just relax. Just give it a minute. It will come to you."

I nod and look around Two Guns, the limestone ruins and the harsh desert. Direction might mean just that. A direction. North, south, east, or west. I-40 goes west to Flagstaff and east to Winslow.

And then it hits me.

"T," I say. "The first letter is a T."

June smiles and gives me an encouraging nod.

I smooth out the remnants of the T-shirt on the dry dirt and write a T in the dust a little bit in front of "e it easy."

I smile because it's so silly. "We're going to Winslow, June," I say, and then cough a bunch. "Dallas is in Winslow."

She looks confused.

"The direction is east," I say. "This shirt said, 'Take it Easy.' An old Eagles song, the one where the singer is stressed out and he's in Winslow, standing on a corner, and he sees a girl driving by and the girl is checking him out."

"Okay..." she says.

I shrug. "Winslow based their whole tourist economy on that

song. There's a couple of statues of the writer of the song, Glenn Frey, and he's standing on the corner, right on Old Route 66. There's a mural of the girl in the old flatbed Ford looking at him."

She nods. "And Dallas is there?"

"Yup," I say. "And Talia is waiting for us... with another trap."

She stands up and brushes her jeans off and extends her hand to me. It's a moment and I give it just a little room. Neither one of us would have survived the Death Cave alone. And there is no apocalypse for me without June anymore.

Sure, it's another trap, but Dallas is one of us. And if playing Talia's "game" is the only way to get her back, the only way to survive, that's exactly what we're going to do.

Together.

EPISODE 10
WOODY AND JUNE VERSUS WINSLOW

More adventure, so many more zombies, and more Woody and June awaits you in.... *Woody and June versus Winslow*. Available 11/2022

To stay abreast of all things Woody and June, head over to WoodyAndJune.com and sign up for my e-mail newsletter and don't miss out on a thing! Plus, you'll get a free ebook that includes "Park's Law of the Apocalypse," a newsletter-exclusive story in the world of Woody and June.

WOODY AND JUNE VERSUS WINSLOW

Isn't Winslow the Place to "Take it Easy"?

Woody Beckman and June Medina defied the odds and found each other in post-zombie-apocalypse Arizona. No longer go-it-alone survivors, they now face the future together with something to lose. Each other.

With Dallas kidnapped and Talia's twisted "game" moving into high gear, can Woody and June do the impossible and save Dallas, survive Winslow, and escape Talia's insidious trap?

Can Woody and June beat the odds and let their love flourish in a world of zombies and psychotic, petty, wannabe warlords?

A story of adventure and love and taking things (even the apocalypse) in stride.

BEFORE YOU GO

Before you go, my book, *Bits, Bites, and Rarities: The Worlds of Robert J. McCarter* is a fantastic introduction to my series and worlds. It's only available to my newsletter subscribers, and the price is the best part. It's free!

This action-packed book contains 15 stories, is 750+ pages long, and has 4 exclusive stories that are not available anywhere else, including "Park's Law of the Apocalypse," a story in the world of Woody and June you can't read anywhere else.

Get it today at *RobertJMcCarter.com/newsletter*

ABOUT THE AUTHOR

Robert J. McCarter is the author of more than ten novels and over a hundred short stories. He is a regular contributor to *Pulphouse Fiction Magazine* and his short fiction has also appeared in *The Saturday Evening Post, Andromeda Spaceways Inflight Magazine, Everyday Fiction,* and numerous anthologies.

Robert writes in a variety of genres from contemporary fantasy to science fiction and just about everything in between. His diverse background—including a career in software engineering, growing up on a ranch riding horses, and acting—colors the stories he tells.

He lives in the mountains of Arizona with his amazing wife and his ridiculously adorable dogs.

Find out more at:
RobertJMcCarter.com

BOOKS BY ROBERT J. MCCARTER

WOODY AND JUNE VERSUS THE APOCALYPSE

For a great deal, pick up *Woody and June Versus the Apocalypse* a volume at at time!

Woody and June Versus the Apocalypse: Volume 1 (Episodes 1 - 7)

- Woody and June versus the Wannabe Warlord
- Woody and June versus the Fungus-Head Zombies
- Woody and June versus the Grand Canyon
- Woody and June versus the Ex
- Woody and June versus the Third Wheel
- Woody and June versus Phantom Company
- Woody and June versus the Daring Rescue

Woody and June Versus the Apocalypse: Volume 2 (Episodes 8 - 12) *Coming 2/2023*

- Woody and June versus the Chase (coming 9/2022)
- Woody and June versus Two Guns (coming 10/2022)
- Woody and June versus Winslow (coming 11/2022)
- Woody and June versus the Infection (coming 12/2022)
- Woody and June versus the Siege (coming 1/2023)

Find out more at WoodyAndJune.com

NEUTRINOMAN & LIGHTNINGIRL: A LOVE STORY

For a great deal, pick up *Neutrinoman & Lightningirl: A Love Story* a season at at time!

Season 1 (Omnibus edition of Episodes 1 - 3)

- Meteor Attack!
- Toxic Asset
- Protocol X

Season 2 (Omnibus edition of Episodes 4-6)

- Off Book
- Hard Times
- Elemental Factors

Find out the latest at Neutrinoman.com

For a complete list of books, go to RobertJMcCarter.com/books